Stan & Julie Hartzler & Family;

With much love from Auntie Susan.

Fondly remembering our day at the
Winnipeg Zoo in the summer of 2014.

Princess

by Dennis Fast

Heartland

Printed by Friesens in Altona, Manitoba, Canada

For Ada and Adam,
and for all those who cherish wildlife
and recognize the need
to preserve it for future generations.

My thanks to the many parents and their children who gave the first draft of this book a resounding thumbs up. Julie and Jeff Thompson of Strait & Level Enterprises, LLC, for their encouragement and financial support to help get this book published. Heartland Associates for taking on the book and bringing it to fruition. Dawn Huck for her exceptional design and layout. Barbara Huck for her editorial suggestions, including the idea to write the story in couplet form. All the polar bears who posed willingly for their portraits on the promise of future fame! Frieda, Stuart, Byron, Val, Ada and Adam, who inspire me to greater things. —Dennis Fast, May 2014

Library and Archives Canada Cataloguing in Publication

Fast, Dennis, 1943-, author
Princess / by Dennis Fast.
ISBN 978-1-896150-79-6 (bound)

I. Title.

PS8611.A794P75 2014   jC813'.6   C2014-903431-8

Heartland Associates would like to thank Manitoba Culture, Heritage and Tourism for its continued assistance and support.

Heartland Associates, Inc.
PO Box 103 RPO Corydon
Winnipeg, MB R3M 3S3

www.heartlandbooks.ca
hrtland@mts.net

ENVIRONMENTAL BENEFITS STATEMENT

Heartland Associates Inc saved the following resources by printing the pages of this book on chlorine free paper made with 10% post-consumer waste.

TREES	WATER	SOLID WASTE	GREENHOUSE GASES
1	511	34	94
FULLY GROWN	GALLONS	POUNDS	POUNDS

Environmental impact estimates were made using the Environmental Paper Network Paper Calculator 3.2. For more information visit www.papercalculator.org.

Here's a story about Princess
just for YOU today

in her cold Arctic home on wild Hudson Bay.

Like a far-away desert that's covered with sand,
the Arctic is a carpet of snow-white land.

Many creatures that live here are white as the snow:

arctic foxes,

willow ptarmigan

Did you know willow ptarmigan turn brown in the summer?

and snowy owls,

you know.

The polar bears, too, are as white as the ice;

But a bear called Princess is especially nice.

Did you know
polar bear hair reflects
light and can look
yellowish or white?

Caribou march by her
and some of them race,

bringing smiles and a laugh
to Princess's face.

Princess laughs

as she rolls

on her snow-white bed,

till she holds her big tummy and squeezes her head.

The foxes come running –
they think she is hurt,

but they laugh with her, too,
when they see her shy smirk.

Winter is coming;
the snowy owls start to fly;

will Princess be alone
or have friends nearby?

Now it's November; the ice and the snow
are calling the bears 'cause they have to go.

Did you know polar bears spend most of the year on the Arctic ice?

They'll be looking for food far out on the Bay
but Princess must go on her own lonely way.

Did you know there are red foxes in the Arctic?

Under deep drifts of snow
she'll make a soft dome,

and dream pleasant dreams
of her warm summer home,

Did you know
polar bear dens can
have two "doors"?

where she loafs in pink fields
of flowers and mosses,

the **hot** summer sun

causing rolls and quick tosses.

She loves being warm and she loves being lazy,
but her dreams always end with the thought of a baby.

Did you know fireweed flowers can be eaten like salad?

One day in March,
Princess bursts through the snow.
Surprise!
She's got company.
What do you know!

There stands tiny Braveheart, as bold as can be,

and then out comes twin
brother. "Hey, look at me!"

The twins are amazed by the sun and the cold,

but they must follow Mother. They're just ten weeks old!

Did you know polar bear babies are called cubs?

Pretty soon they are playing
with trees their own size
and a taller one quickly becomes
Braveheart's prize.

Wimpy tries to steal it, then complains to his mother,

but she softly says,
"Wimpy, please play with your brother."

"It's always more fun than fighting you know,
and you have to be friends; we've a long way to go."

"I'm the king of the castle,"
boasts Braveheart, "Ho, ho!"

Now who must share?
Do you think that you know?

Princess soon calls them
to go for a walk;

they'll learn about sharing
after a soft, gentle talk.

She settles them down
near the edge of a willow,

where she'll feed them and warm them
and become their soft pillow.

Braveheart and Wimpy
dive in for their dinner

with no need to worry about
who is the winner.

They feed and they play
till it dizzies their head.
"Good night," Braveheart waves,
"I'm going to bed."

"Good night," Princess says,
as she gets a sweet kiss,
But Wimpy seems grouchy.
Is something amiss?

Did you know cubs stay with their mothers for up to three years?

A cuddle soon warms them
and makes them feel snug

with their momma a blanket,
as well as a rug.

Pretty soon they are nodding,
bidding all "Nighty, night."

As the stars and aurora
dance away out of sight.

You can see they're asleep,
and you should be, too.

Do you think
that the twins
are now dreaming
of YOU?

Polar Bear Activity Page

1. Name three animals or birds that polar bears share their arctic land with:

_____

2. What do polar bears call their home? What special feature does it often have?

_____

3. At what age do polar bear cubs typically leave their den with their mother? _____

4. What does Princess like to do in the summer? _____

Can you draw an arctic scene?